# Winter, Spring, Summer, Fall…

*Snowshoe Hare*

a HARE'S hair changes with them all.

With
love
to
PAUL
and
PHILIP

Reinforced binding of hardcover edition suitable for library use.

Copyright © 1982 by Ruth Heller. All rights reserved.
Published by Grosset & Dunlap, Inc.,
a member of The Putnam & Grosset Group, New York.
Published simultaneously in Canada. Sandcastle Books
and the Sandcastle logo are trademarks belonging to The Putnam & Grosset Group.
GROSSET & DUNLAP is a trademark of Grosset & Dunlap, Inc.
First Sandcastle Books edition, 1993. Printed in Singapore.
Library of Congress Catalog Card Number: 82-80872

ISBN (hardcover) 0-448-01822-5   1993 Printing

ISBN (Sandcastle) 0-448-40453-2   B C D E F G H I J

# ANIMALS BORN ALIVE AND WELL

## BY RUTH HELLER

*House Mouse*

Publishers • GROSSET & DUNLAP • New York

MAMMALS
are
animals with fur or hair
who nurse their young
and breathe fresh air.

They don't lay eggs
except these two.
These are the only
two who do.

*Spiny Anteater*

*Duckbill Platypus*

They don't lay eggs, as I have said, they're born alive and well instead.

*African Elephants*

Sometimes a
MAMMAL'S
hair
is scant,
as
on
the
thick-
skinned
ELEPHANT.

*Pekinese*

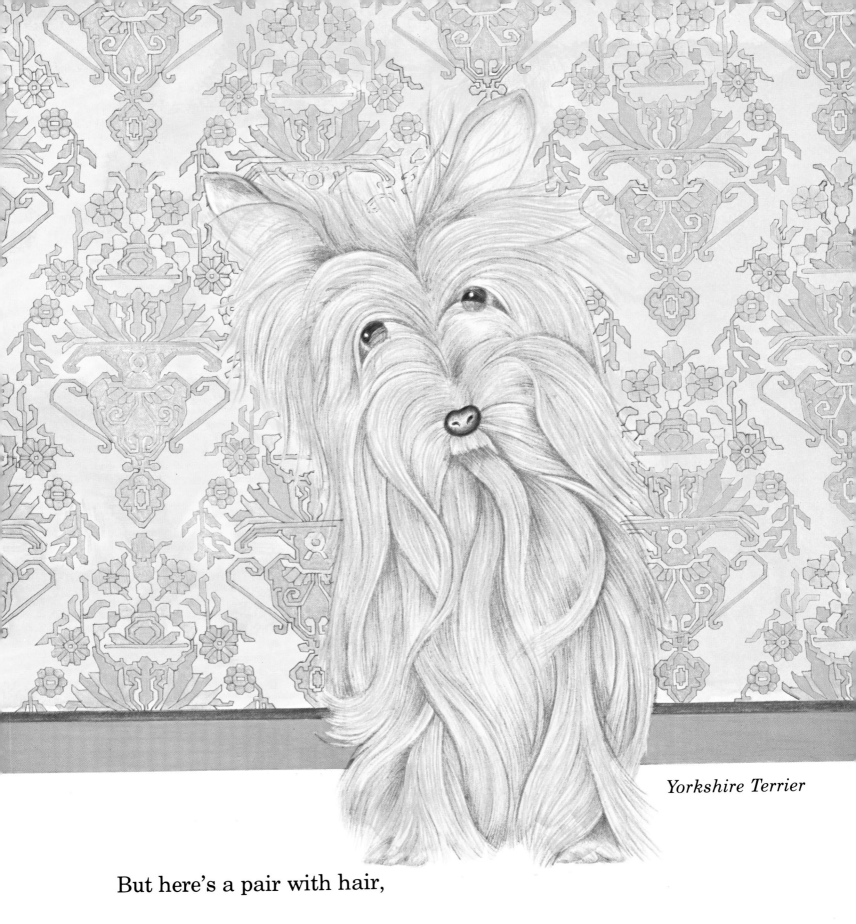

*Yorkshire Terrier*

But here's a pair with hair,

Okapi

Zebra

Ring-tailed
Lemur

and
here
are
lots
with
stripes
and
spots.

*Giraffe*

*Cloud
Leopard*

*Leopard*

*Tiger*

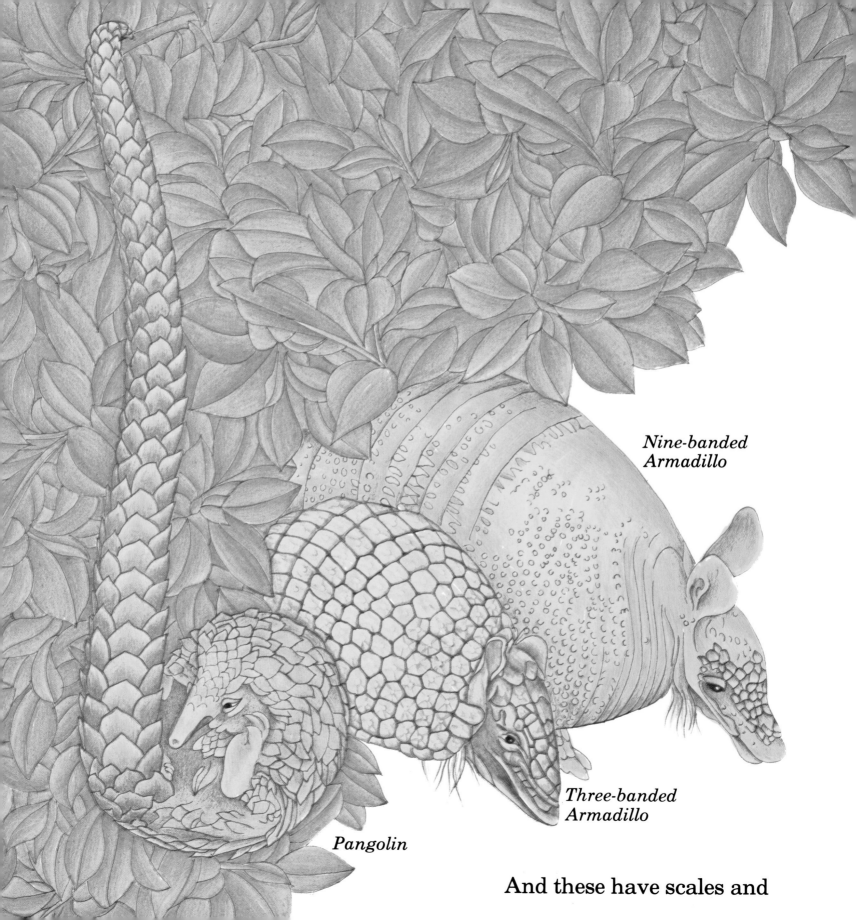

*Nine-banded Armadillo*

*Three-banded Armadillo*

*Pangolin*

And these have scales and

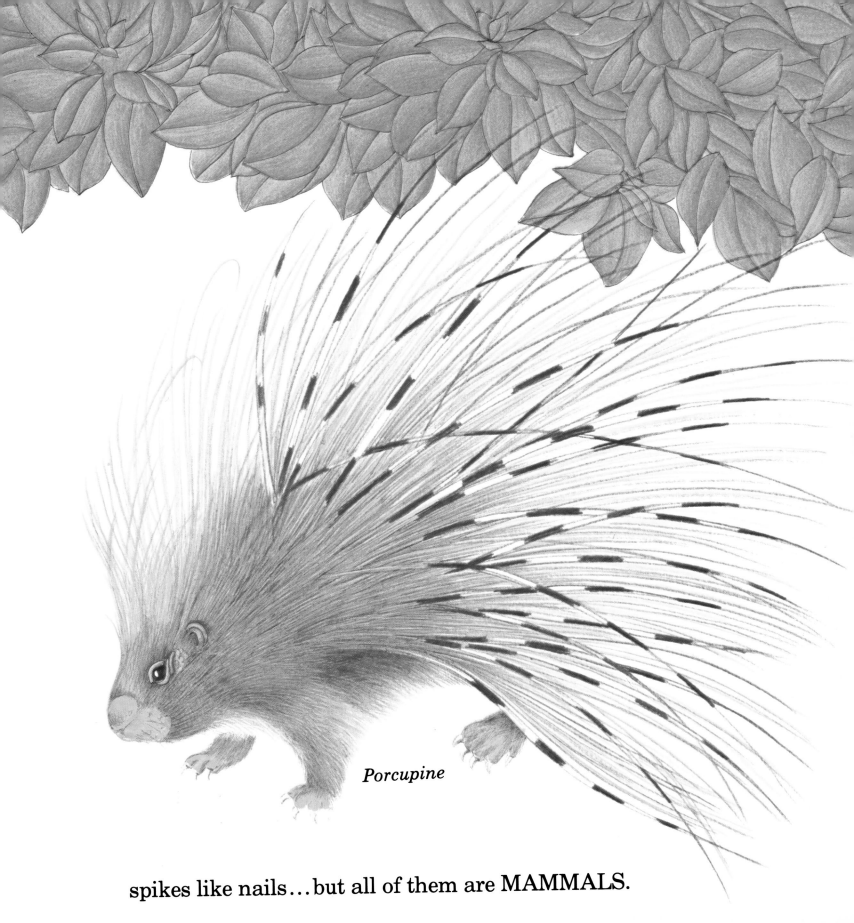

*Porcupine*

spikes like nails…but all of them are MAMMALS.

So are
CAMELS,

and like all the others,
they are nourished
by
their
mothers.

Dromedaries

Gazelle

MAMMALS
wild
and…

*Deer*

*Stoat*

# MAMMALS
tame

all do more or less the same.

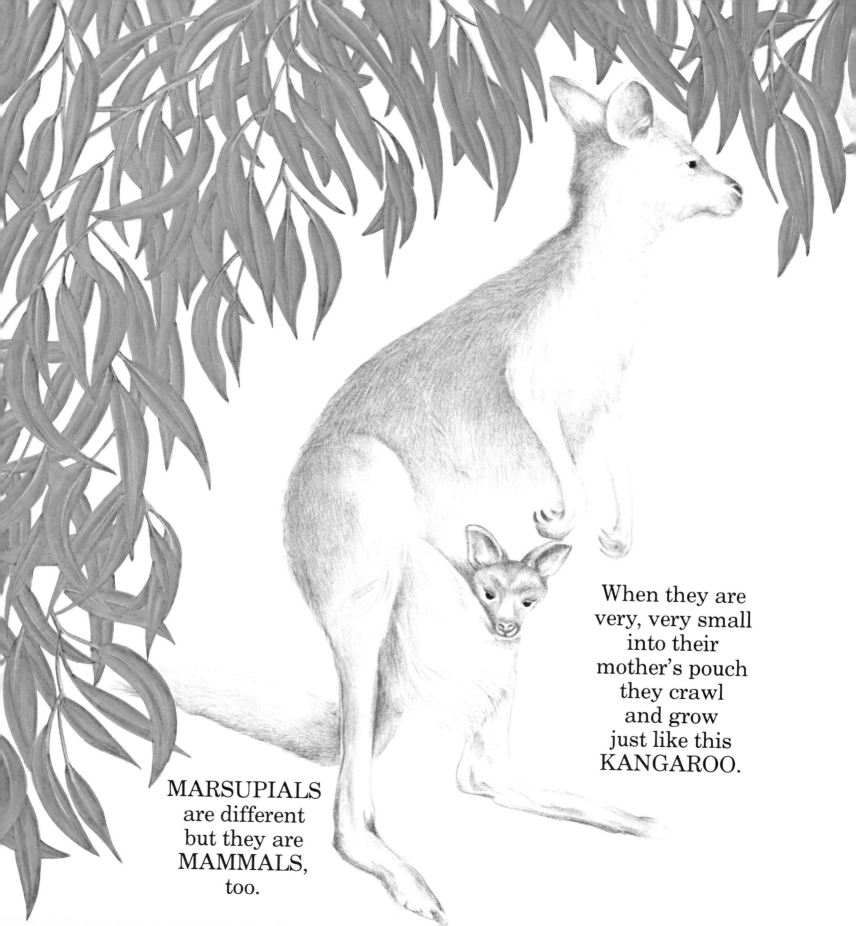

When they are
very, very small
into their
mother's pouch
they crawl
and grow
just like this
KANGAROO.

MARSUPIALS
are different
but they are
MAMMALS,
too.

KOALAS
are
MARSUPIALS, too.

MAMMALS
all
breathe air,
you
understand.

*Moose*

*Bighorn Sheep*

*Mandrill*

*Panda*

This
isn't
hard
for
those
on
land,
or
even
those
found…

*Guinea Pig*

*Rhinoceros*

*Hare*

*Aardvark*

*Kangaroo Rat*

*Weasel*

*Squirrel*

Fallow Deer

Wild Goat

Bison

Red Fox

Hippopotamus

Giant Anteater

Prairie Dog

underground...

Mole

Shrew Mole

or those who fly,

*Bat*

or climb up high.

Marmoset

Tarsier

Gibbon

Baboon

*Sloth*

*Bush Baby*

*Gibbon*

*Spider Monkey*

But MAMMALS living in the sea

*Porpoise*

*Sperm Whale*

*Walrus*

*Seal*

have to surface frequently.

Sea Otter

Dolphin

Manatee

Narwhal

*Porpoise*

The
PORPOISE,
WHALE,
and
MANATEE
have their babies
in the sea.

Humpback Whale

Manatee

The
WALRUS,
SEAL,
and
OTTER
prefer to
leave the
water.

*Otter*

*Walrus*

*Seal*

*Walrus*

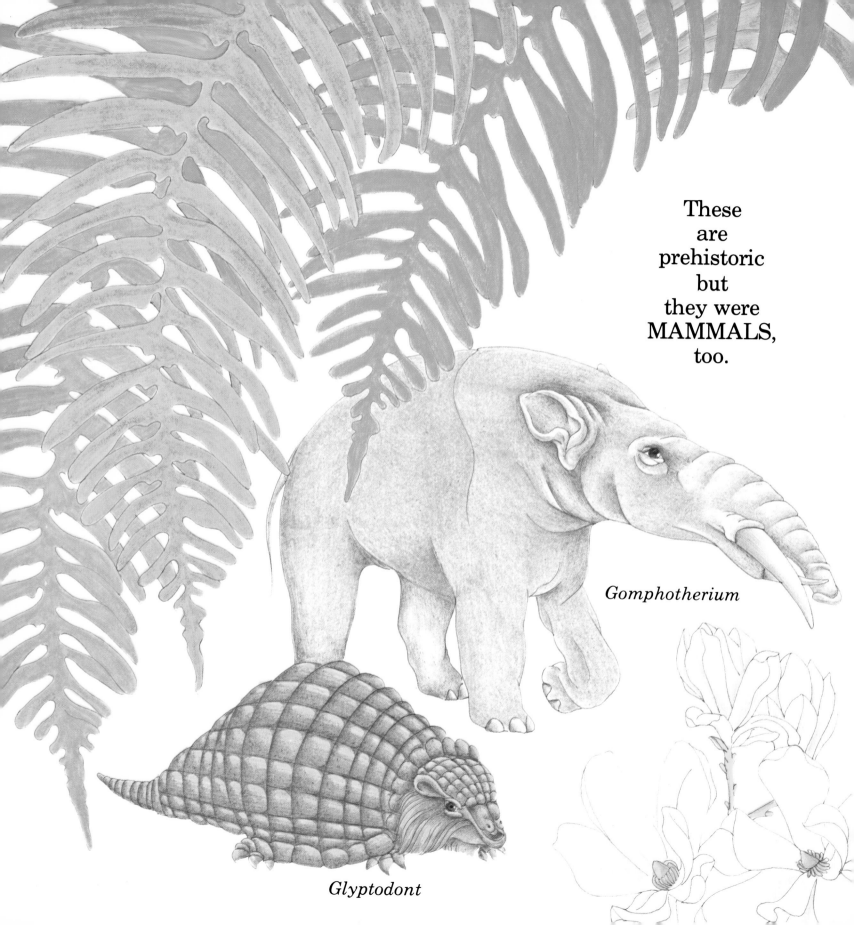

These
are
prehistoric
but
they were
MAMMALS,
too.

*Gomphotherium*

*Glyptodont*

Their names
are very
long indeed
and
may be
very hard
to read.

Baluchitherium

Macrauchenia

The
largest
MAMMAL
is
the
BLUE WHALE.

The
smallest
is
the
SHREW.

*Shrew*

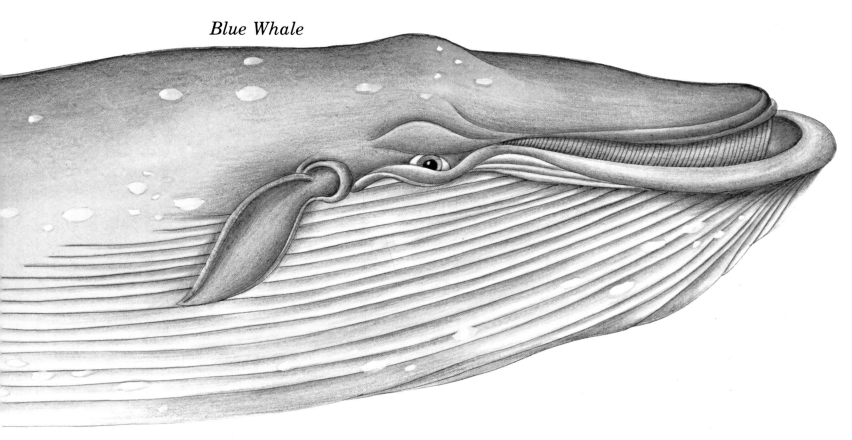

*Blue Whale*

The best of all are…

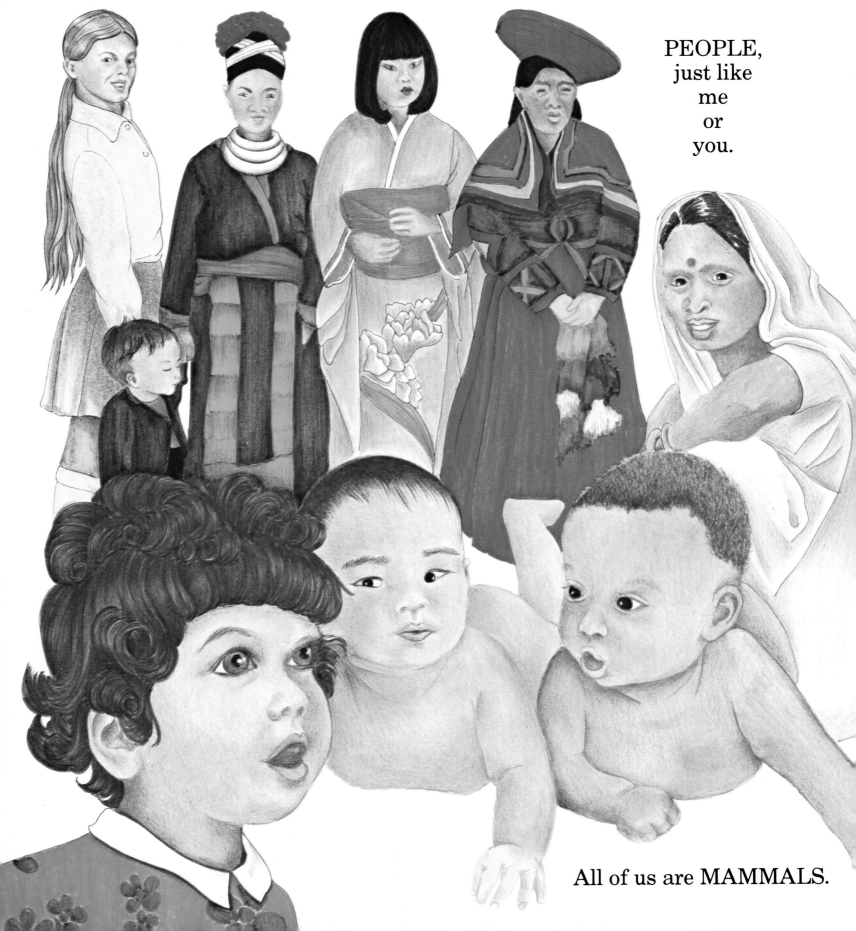

PEOPLE,
just like
me
or
you.

All of us are MAMMALS.

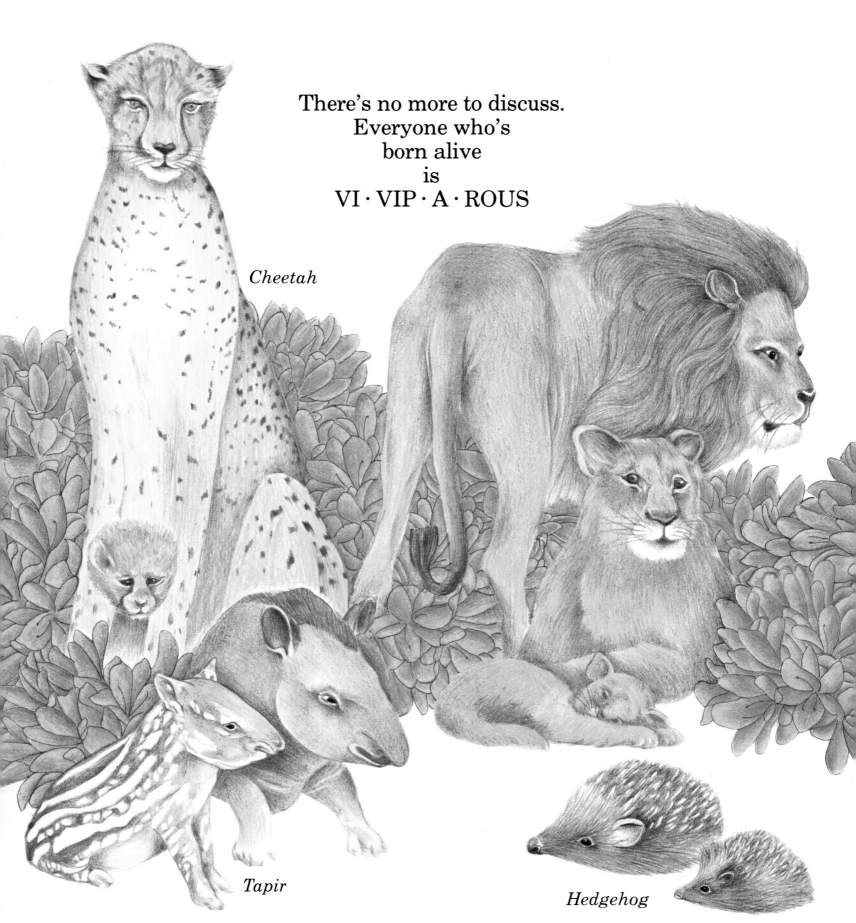

There's no more to discuss.
Everyone who's
born alive
is
VI · VIP · A · ROUS

Cheetah

Tapir

Hedgehog

Sheep

Horse

Pig

Winter, Spring, Summer, Fall…

*Snowshoe Hare*

a HARE'S hair changes with them all.